Dear Parent:
Your child's love of reading starts here!

Every child learns to read in a different way and at his or her own speed. Some go back and forth between reading levels and read favorite books again and again. Others read through each level in order. You can help your young reader improve and become more confident by encouraging his or her own interests and abilities. From books your child reads with you to the first books he or she reads alone, there are I Can Read Books for every stage of reading:

SHARED READING
Basic language, word repetition, and whimsical illustrations, ideal for sharing with your emergent reader

BEGINNING READING
Short sentences, familiar words, and simple concepts for children eager to read on their own

READING WITH HELP
Engaging stories, longer sentences, and language play for developing readers

READING ALONE
Complex plots, challenging vocabulary, and high-interest topics for the independent reader

ADVANCED READING
Short paragraphs, chapters, and exciting themes for the perfect bridge to chapter books

I Can Read Books have introduced children to the joy of reading since 1957. Featuring award-winning authors and illustrators and a fabulous cast of beloved characters, I Can Read Books set the standard for beginning readers.

A lifetime of discovery begins with the magical words **"I Can Read!"**

Visit www.icanread.com for information
on enriching your child's reading experience.

I Can Read Book® is a trademark of HarperCollins Publishers.

Superman: Day of Doom
Copyright © 2013 DC Comics.
SUPERMAN and all related characters and elements are trademarks of and © DC Comics.
(s13)

HARP28603
Printed in the United States of America. No part of this book may be used or reproduced in any manner whatsoever without written permission except in the case of brief quotations embodied in critical articles and reviews. For information address HarperCollins Children's Books, a division of HarperCollins Publishers, 10 East 53rd Street, New York, NY 10022.
www.harpercollinschildrens.com

Library of Congress catalog card number: 2012956519
ISBN 978-0-06-221001-2

Book design by John Sazaklis

14 15 16 17 18   LP/WOR   10 9 8 7 6 5 4 3 2   ❖   First Edition

SUPERMAN
Day of Doom

by John Sazaklis
pictures by Andy Smith
colors by Brad Vancata

SUPERMAN created by Jerry Siegel and Joe Shuster

HARPER
An Imprint of HarperCollinsPublishers

CLARK KENT

Clark Kent is a
newspaper reporter.
He is secretly Superman.

LOIS LANE

Lois Lane is also a
newspaper reporter.
She works for the
Daily Planet newspaper.

JIMMY OLSEN

Jimmy Olsen is a
photographer. He works
with Clark and Lois for the
Daily Planet newspaper.

SUPERMAN

Superman has many amazing powers.
He was born on the planet Krypton.

DOOMSDAY

The perfect killing machine, each time
Doomsday is defeated, he comes back
stronger than before.

Deep in an underground vault,

a monster struggles.

This alien criminal was imprisoned

to protect the people of Earth.

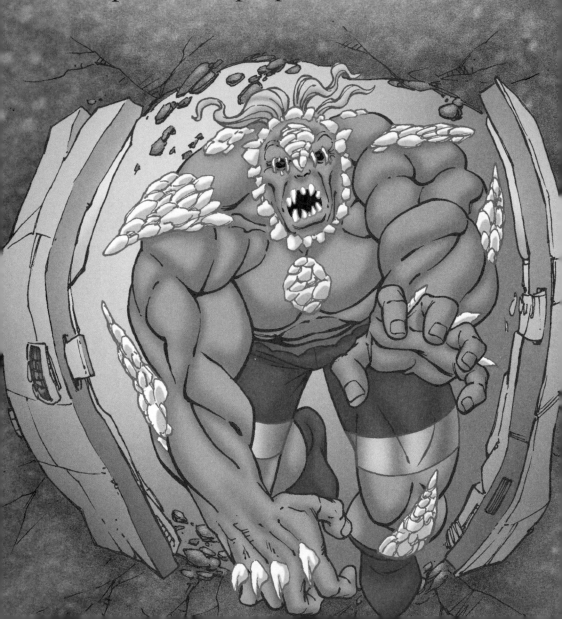

Now free, Doomsday sets off

on a path of destruction.

His targets are Metropolis

and its protector, Superman!

At the Daily Planet Building,

the news team is hard at work.

Suddenly, BOOM!

The walls begin to shake.

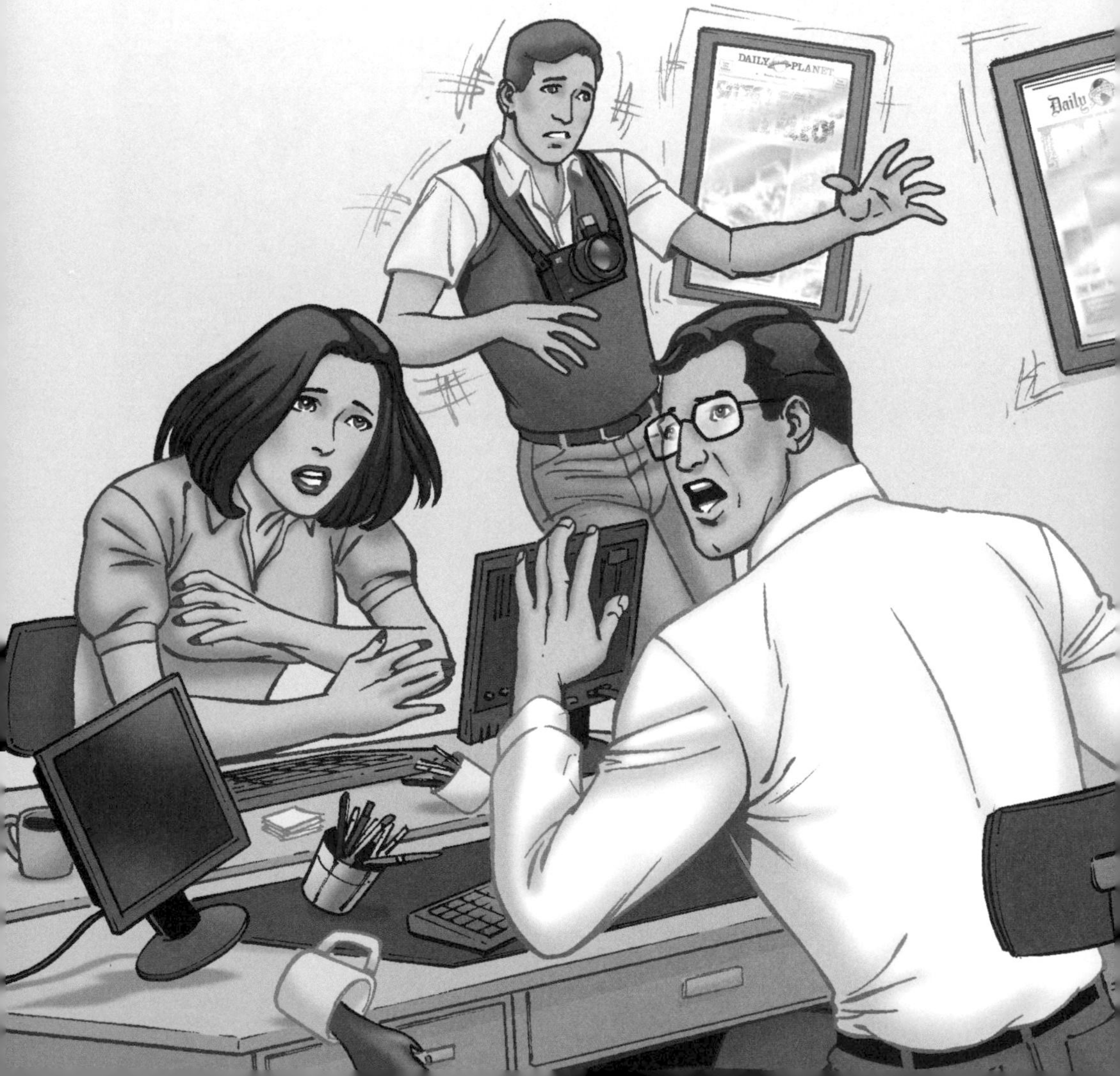
DAILY PLANET
Daily

"What was that?" Lois asks.

Perry White exits his office.

"That's our front page story,"

he yells. "Go get it!"

Clark uses his X-ray vision.

He sees the cause of the rumble.

It is a large, rampaging creature!

Lois and Jimmy run to the elevator.

"Where are you going, Mr. Kent?"

Jimmy asks Clark.

"Elevators make me nervous,"

replies Clark. "I'll take the stairs."

With his friends gone,

Clark changes into his alter ego.

"This looks like a job for Superman!"

Doomsday tears through the city.

He stomps on cars with his feet.

He rips lampposts out of the ground.

In a blur of red and blue,

Superman appears.

"Your trail of terror ends here,"

says the Man of Steel.

Doomsday charges forward.

Superman attacks back.

The two titans clash but they are

equally matched.

"If I can't defeat this villain with strength," Superman says, "then I'll have to use speed!"

The Man of Steel breaks his grasp

and zips behind Doomsday.

He catches the villain off guard.

Superman punches Doomsday

into an abandoned parking garage.

The building collapses onto the beast.

KA-BOOM!

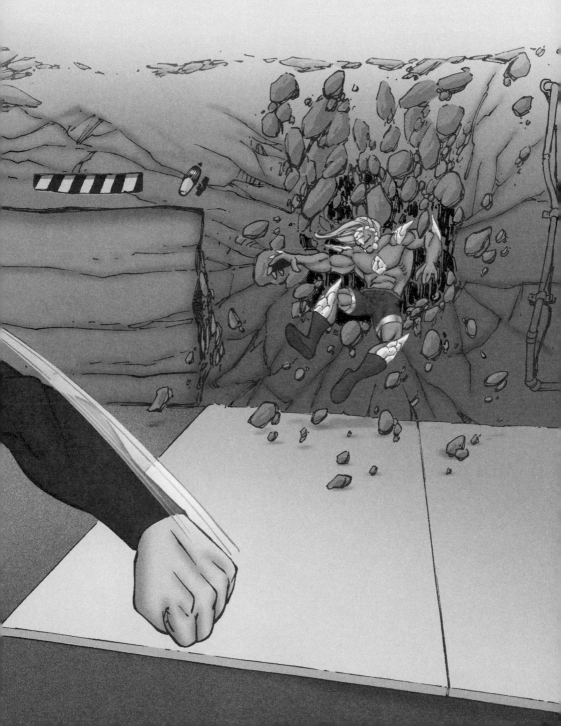

Lois and Jimmy run to Superman.

"You did it," Lois says.

"You saved the day!" Jimmy adds.

The young reporter snaps pictures.

Behind them, the rubble moves.

A massive fist rams through,

followed by the rest of Doomsday.

The monster roars with rage.

Doomsday leaps high into the air.
He lands on Superman and
pounds him into the pavement.
SMASH!

With the Man of Steel lost underground,

Doomsday turns to face the reporters.

"Uh-oh," Lois says. "RUN!"

She grabs Jimmy and sprints for safety.

Superman flies out of the crater

and sees his friends in danger.

"If strength and speed aren't enough,"

says the hero, "I'll have to use smarts."

He aims his heat vision

at the street, and he fires.

The asphalt begins to melt, and

Doomsday sinks into the street.

"Just returning the favor, big fella,"

Superman says to Doomsday.

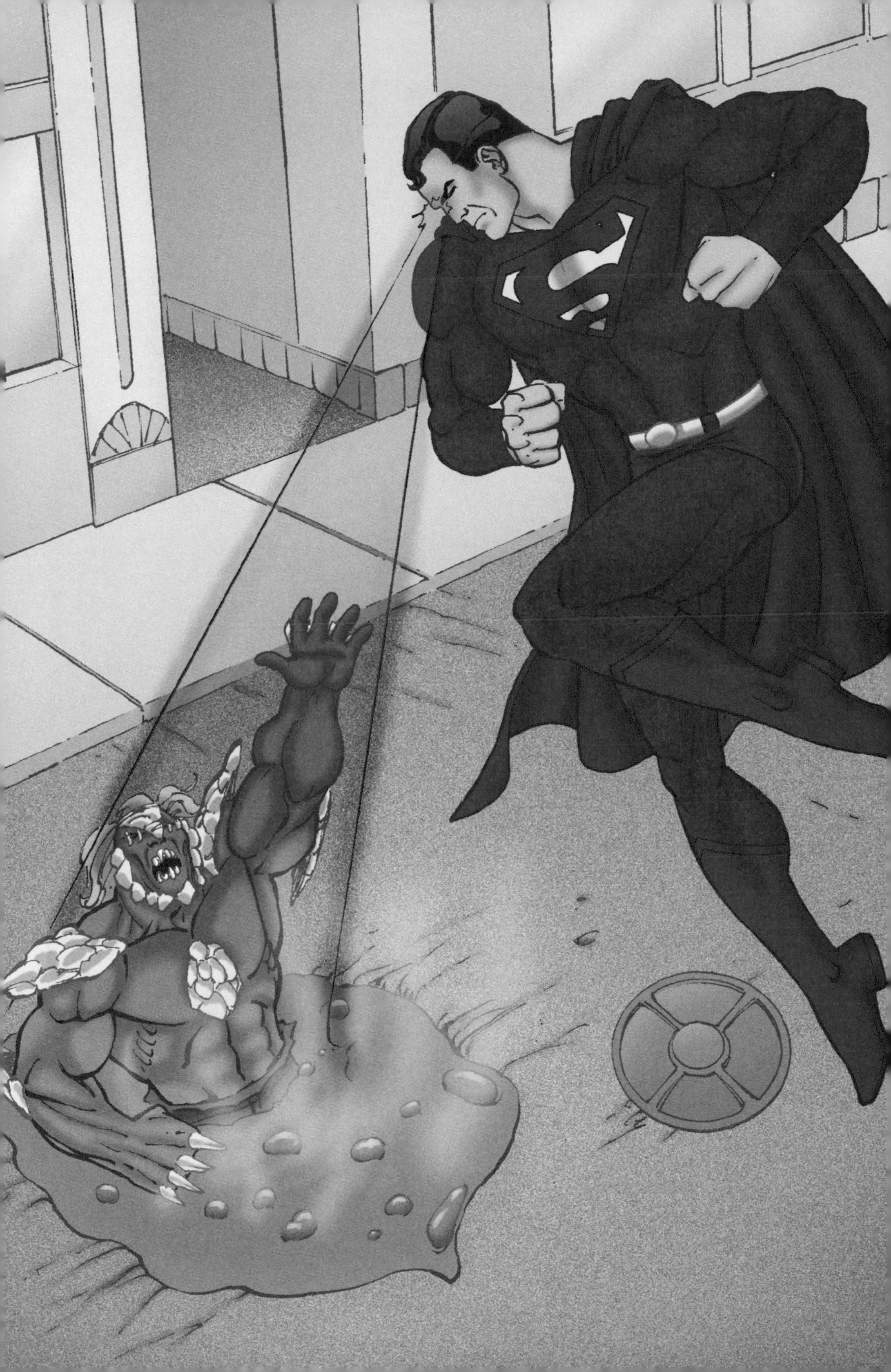

Superman uses his freezing breath

to quickly cool the hot asphalt.

The monster is temporarily trapped.

"You need to chill out," says Superman.

Then he flies as fast as he can

to his Fortress of Solitude.

That is where the Man of Steel

keeps artifacts from his home planet.

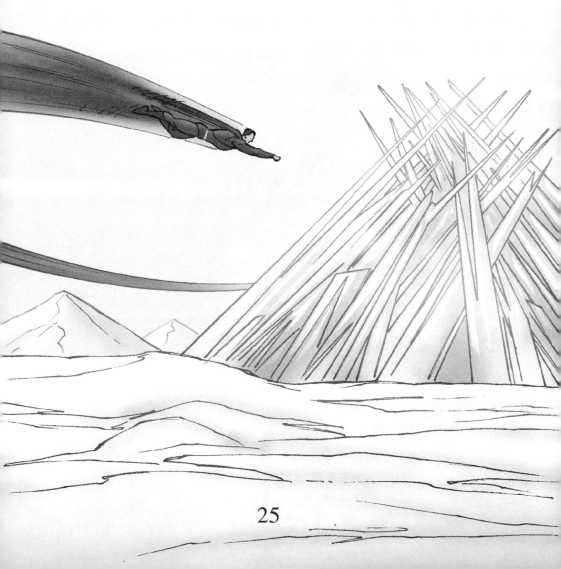

At the Fortress, Superman
picks up a special device.
It is the Phantom Zone Projector.
The Projector sends criminals to the
Phantom Zone, an outer space prison.

"Too bad you're not as fast

as Superman," Jimmy adds.

"Too bad," Clark says, and smiles.

"I bet you got a great story to tell!"

Then the hero waves and flies away.

Seconds later, Clark Kent

stumbles out of the Daily Planet Building.

"Phew! That building has WAY

too many stairs." Clark gasps.

"Did I miss anything?"

"You sure did, Clark," Lois says.

Lois and Jimmy thank Superman
for saving the city once again.
"It is my sworn duty,"
Superman says.

Suddenly, Superman reappears!

"Your day of doom is over," he says.

He zaps Doomsday with the device.

In a flash, the villain is gone.

In the city, Doomsday breaks free.

He heads for the Daily Planet Building.

Will Superman be too late?

The Man of Steel then zooms
from the Arctic back to Metropolis.
WHOOSH!